THE SURPRISE WITNESS:
An Apologia for Adam and Eve

LINDA LEE MURRELL

THE SURPRISE WITNESS: An Apologia for Adam and Eve

Concept Visionary: Bishop Dr. Johnny Ray Youngblood

Cover Design: Jo Anne Meekins as envisioned by the author

Scriptures are taken from the King James Version of the Bible
unless otherwise indicated.

Inspired 4 U Publications
Publisher@inspired4uministries.com
www.howtoselfpublishinexcellence.com

ISBN-13: 979-8-9859571-0-5

DEDICATION

I dedicate this book to God; my beloved Mother, Edith Theusdee McGowan; visionary Bishop Dr. Johnny Ray Youngblood; and Queen Mother Sarah Plowden.

Thank you, God, for blessing me with my mother, who is my mentor and best friend. Thank you, God, for also giving me the gift of writing. Writing has allowed me to express myself freely and has become exceedingly cathartic.

Thank you, mom, for encouraging me during every event and goal I had in life. You taught me to trust God and that there were no limitations.

Thank you, Bishop Dr. Johnny Ray Youngblood, for trusting me with your vision.

Thank you, Queen Mother Sarah Plowden, for giving the "Sisters of Esther" women's group the assignment of writing an *Apology to the Black Man*. My journey as a writer and critical thinker began in 1987 through this writing assignment.

CONTENTS:

¹³ Thou hast been in Eden the garden of God; every precious stone was thy covering, the sardius, topaz, and the diamond, the beryl, the onyx, and the jasper, the sapphire, the emerald, and the carbuncle, and gold: the workmanship of thy tabrets and of thy pipes was prepared in thee in the day that thou wast created.

(Ezekiel 28:13, KJV)

FOREWORD

Since human relationships, particularly between Men and Women, are measured and monitored by the Genesis story, we felt led to look in-depth from another angle through more experienced <u>EYES TO SEE AND HEAR</u> what God allows the Genesis incident to teach.

The open mind is susceptible to the truth as to falsehood, so since closed minds tend to be the basic mindset of many Christians; and since the closed-minded conclusions answer few questions and raise hardly any, we decided to get together and question **ANEW**.

— *Bishop Dr. Johnny Ray Youngblood*, Concept Visionary, Executive Pastor/ Spiritual Engineer at Mount Pisgah Baptist Church in Brooklyn and Queens, New York

[14] *Thou art the anointed cherub that covereth; and I have set thee so: thou wast upon the holy mountain of God; thou hast walked up and down in the midst of the stones of fire.*

(Ezekiel 28:14, KJV)

PREFACE

APOLOGIA IS A GREEK WORD MEANING "EXPLANATION"

An **apologia** (Latin for apology, from Greek "speaking in defense") is a formal defense of an opinion, position or action. The term's current use, often in the context of religion, theology and philosophy, derives from Justin Martyr's *First Apology* (AD 155–157) and was later employed by John Henry Newman's *Apologia Pro Vita Sua* (English: *A Defense of* One's *Own Life*) of 1864, which presented a formal defense of the history of his Christian life, leading to his acceptance by the Catholic Church in 1845. In modern usage, *apologia* describes a formal defense and should not be confused with the sense of the word 'apology' as an expression of regret; however, apology may mean apologia, depending on the context of use.

— Wikipedia, the free encyclopedia

THE GAP THEORY

During the study of Genesis, the Think Tank Nucleus group learned about the Gap Theory, which teaches that **a long time elapsed between the verses in Genesis 1:1 and 1:2.** The Gap Theory was proposed in 1814 by Thomas Chalmers (1780-1847), a Scottish Minister and Professor of Theology.

Many gap theorists point to the book of Ezekiel 28:13-15 as describing the original creation before the desolation of Genesis 1:2. The passage speaks of Satan dwelling in Eden, the Garden of God, before sin had infected it.

In this book, you may see references to the Gap Theory. It is a theory that many religious leaders and Pastors have concluded differently regarding its validity.

WHY THE THINK TANK?

The Think Tank-Genesis Nucleus was a group of men and women members of St. Paul Community Baptist Church at its inception. Some, like me, are still active members.

The Think Tank members shared varied educational, spiritual, and life experiences. They held various leadership roles and served as laypersons, ministers, Levitical staff members, and Elders. One common ground that all Think Tank members shared was a commitment to the ministry of Jesus Christ and the edification of the people of God and those in the community beyond the walls of St. Paul.

The Think Tank came together in 2003 with a prayerful spirit to ponder the Genesis passage and have an open mind about the demise of male-female relationships. All members shared the common goal of healing our relationships. Many of us had to put aside preconceived notions and past hurts to uncover the root cause of symptoms plaguing male-female relationships today.

If I had a million dollars to give each member, it would not be enough to express the joy I felt every time I left a session with them. Their commitment and love for this project confirmed that God chose this group, not me. Even though we challenged each other, the Think Tank differed from other male-female discussions because hostility and blaming never occurred.

The men in our sessions brilliantly dissected the scripture. God's image and likeness became flesh before us in Bishop Dr. Johnny Ray Youngblood, Elder David Miller, Elder Ronald Hudson, Rev. Lesley Shannon, and Clay Fielding. I thank God for them all. The original Adam would be proud of how they represented Black Manhood. I love them all.

The women in our sessions, Queen Mother Sarah Plowden, Gloria Miller, Hakikah Shamsiden, Carrie Simmons, Hanifah Ama (Helen Parilla), Ummi Modeste, Gwen Warner, Lula Staples, Miriam Fauntleroy, Charlene Caldwell, and Brenda K. Nealy, took discernment to a new level. I can honestly say that we listened. There were times when we listened to the men, times when we prayed, and a time when we challenged, but never with an argumentative tone.

The desired balance between men and women was evident during our sessions. For example: as with the analogy of an intimate sexual act between man and woman, the men deposited knowledge during some sessions, and the women received it. At other times, there was a mutual exchange. There was no competitiveness, only a genuine search for the truth of what happened in the Garden of Eden.

In 2003, I posed the following charge to the Think Tank based on Esther 4:14b (KJV) *"Who knoweth whether thou art come to the kingdom for such a time as this"*:

We have gathered for such a time as this to participate in healing our relationships, break the Willie Lynch cycle, and restore ourselves to our original natural state.

The Genesis Nucleus Think Tank Members

Bishop Dr. Johnny Ray Youngblood, Linda Lee Murrell, Queen Mother Sarah Plowden, Hakikah Shamsiden, Miriam Fauntleroy, Charlene Caldwell, Gloria Miller, Hanifah Ama Parrilla, Carrie Bell Simmons, R. Ummi Modeste, Brenda K. Nealy, Gwen Warner, Lula Staples, Elder David Miller, Elder Ronald Hudson, Rev. Lesley Shannon, Clay Fielding.

ACKNOWLEDGMENTS

Thank you, family, for your support and confirming that I am creative.

Thank you, Pastor Dr. David K. Brawley, for challenging us continuously as leaders and helping us to imagine something new.

Thank you, Prayer Intercessors: Donna Jo Matthews, Renee M. Mohammed, Gwendolyn Warner, the late Clydetta McKoy, Queen Mother Sarah Plowden, Elder David Miller, Elder Ronald Hudson, and Clay Fielding. I know God has blessed you for interceding on my behalf.

The Holy Spirit led me to ask you to become my prayer intercessors. Some of you asked, "Why me?" I did not have an answer to give at the time but responded that you should ask God because flesh did not direct me to ask you. I know that you brought a new dimension to the Think Tank meetings with your responses and by praying with me at the oddest times. Thank you for taking on the challenge!

Thank you, my dearest Miriam Fauntleroy. You have continued to be my support and friend throughout my writing journey. I thank God for your prayers and your encouragement. I Love you, my sister!

Thank you, my faithful friends; you know who you are. You have continued to play an essential role in my life.

Thank you, Publisher Jo Anne Meekins, for investing in me with your time, energy, prayers, support, editing, and encouragement. I pray this is just the beginning of our journey together as writer and publisher.

INTRODUCTION

St. Paul Community Baptist Church premiered "THE SURPRISE WITNESS: An Apologia for Adam and Eve" as a play on Saturday, April 29, 2006.

On March 18-22, 2007, the theatre production of this play was presented on stage at the Gaylord Texan Resort and Convention Center.

"THE SURPRISE WITNESS: An Apologia for Adam and Eve" is a therapeutic, psycho-dramatic presentation that looks at the devastating state of our relationships; and takes a non-traditional look at what may have gone wrong in the Garden of Eden.

In this psycho-dramatic presentation, we suggest that there was an intentional conspiracy against God's will for man and woman and that they were initially Black. Our present contention is that this demonic conspiracy manifests itself through white supremacy and racism; and this plot has had continuous seasons of success.

This presentation seeks not to blame man or woman but instead looks at Satan's part in deceiving them. It looks at how Satan conjured up the entire deception in the Garden, using man and woman to get at God.

I am not a theologian or Bible Scholar; I only seek for my writing to create a dialogue among everyone; and that you look at this body of work through an open lens.

I am a Believer in Jesus Christ and have committed to serving Him with my life. Through my consecrated imagination, I interpret and share this story.

The following expresses my creative excerpted version of Genesis 1:1-2, 26; 2:16, 18; and chapter 3.

God's power created many entities for good. Out of nothing, God created wonderfulness; and God's Spirit was ever-present in the midst of creation. God is the Creator, so we, His children, are creators through our DNA.

God was never alone. He and His partners (The Trinity) were together from the beginning of creation. God said, "Let us make man." The "us" refers to the Father, Son, and Holy Spirit.

In God's highest form of creativity was man, and in His genius, He also formed a complementary being for man. God created a Paradise for Adam and Eve to dwell, and He provided everything they needed. They had eternal life and were allowed to freely eat from any tree except the one in the middle of the Garden, and God, not being a dictator, gave them *free will.*

Another of God's creations, a peculiar presence, was also in the Garden. This entity was not innocent like Adam and Eve. He was a trickster, cunning and deceitful. He demonstrated true evil, seeking to destroy humankind, and has continued this mission throughout time.

This deceiver seduced Eve into disobedience and God cursed man and woman, for Adam was with Eve during this encounter and was responsible for his family. Then, God excommunicated them from the Garden.

Every one will pay a price for disobedience. I invite you to reflect and discuss how this story affects our current relationships and determine who you are in this story.

[45]And so it is written, The first man Adam was made a living soul; the last Adam was made a quickening spirit.

(1 Corinthians 15:45, KJV)

1. WHO ARE ADAM AND EVE?

I am Adam. The Creator made me from the dust of the earth and breathed life into me. I became a living being, a man of flesh, but with God's Spirit. God trusted me to take charge of the Garden filled with gold and onyx stone; and the four riverheads, the Pishon, the Gihon, the Hiddekel, and the Euphrates. Paradise is what I am experiencing; yes, this is Paradise.

God said, "I give you reign, and you may eat freely from every tree in the Garden, except the one positioned in the middle. You must not eat from the tree of the knowledge of good and evil, for when you eat from it, YOU WILL SURELY DIE!"

I had everything I needed with only one limitation. What a Gracious God he is. God also said, "Adam, my son, it is not good for man to be alone. I will make a perfect, sinless, suitable companion for you."

God caused me to fall into a deep sleep as He performed a flawless surgery and took one of my ribs to make my helpmate. And in His infinite wisdom, God connected us as one.

This process illustrates God's original plan for a man to have a woman by his side.

I called her woman because she came out of a man. This beautiful specimen is from my bone, and we are one flesh. Upon seeing her, Adam grinned widely in deep gratitude and complete satisfaction.

Afterward, God and I had a conversation. What was it like taking instruction from my Creator? God was clear and direct.

"Adam, I can see you are pleased, but with this gift comes responsibility. You are to cover and protect her and make sure she understands what will happen if she is disobedient. Do you have any questions, my son?"

It seemed so simple; I never felt any questions were necessary. Could I go back and ask questions later if I needed to? I never thought about it. I was in a moment of bliss. In this euphoric state, what could go wrong?

No one could argue that this was Paradise, man communing with his God.

How did we get from Paradise to where we are now?

2. THE FALL OF MAN AND WOMAN

God called out to Adam and asked, "Where are you?" Adam replied, "I heard you in the Garden and was afraid because I was naked, so I hid. "Who told you, you were naked?" questioned God, "Did you eat the fruit from that tree I told you not to eat from?" Adam responded by saying, "The woman you gave me as a companion gave me fruit from the tree, and, yes, I did eat."

Directing His attention to Eve, God asked, "Woman, what have you done?" "The serpent seduced me, and I ate from the tree," she responded, cringing under God's anger and disappointment in man, as thunder and lightning simultaneously resonated through the universe.

God turned to the serpent and said, "Because you have done this awful thing, you are CURSED! On your belly, you will live." *Why would God put the serpent on his belly? This posture change indicates that the serpent was walking before the Fall.* God continued, 'I will make you and the woman hate each other; her offspring and yours will always be enemies. Her

3

offspring will crush your head, and you will bite her offspring's heel."

God further stated to Adam, "Since you listened to your wife, cursed is the ground, and you will sweat working it."

Don't our men work hard; they continuously look forward to making a living. Due to institutionalized racism, our men often work hard but never get to where they want to be. They cannot find their raison d'etre (reason for being, purpose).

To Eve, God said, "Woman, I will increase your pain in childbirth. Your desire will be for your husband, and he will overpower you. You are both banished from the Garden of Eden, and I will place Cherubim and a flaming sword to guard the way to the tree of life."

As you read how this scene unfolds, why do you think God placed Cherubim in front of the tree of life? Could it be God, being the loving God he is, did not want Adam and Eve to live in this sinful state eternally? God knew He had already provided a way out through Jesus Christ before the situation occurred.

3. INTRODUCTION OF SATANS:
Do you really know who they are?

*I*n Satan's attempt to imitate God, he replicates himself into the Satan Trio: Master Satan, She-Devil, Flunky-Deceiver. He and the other Fallen Angels increased their earthly influence as Sons of God when they saw that the daughters of men were beautiful and pleasing to the eye and then intermarried with all they chose. *(Genesis 6:2)*

The Satan Trio exclaims in unison, "WE MESSED UP!"

"I blew it!" Master Satan declares, "Yet you so-called humans complain about minor catastrophes in your life, like divorce, loss of a loved one, sickness, loss of a job, and lack of money. Yeah, those are minor catastrophes. However, I messed up, not just for a lifetime but an eternity. For humanity, there is always hope. But for me, who at one time had it all, there is no hope. Hope is not a part of my existence.

"But I am running ahead of myself; let me stop here and start from the beginning. You see, I have plenty of time. You can sleep if you want to because that is what I want you to do. I want you to remain anesthetized," laughed Master Satan sinisterly. "Demon of Sleep, overcome the people reading this book so that they can miss the diabolical truth of what I am saying."

Master Satan continues contemptuously, "I always see you praying, carrying your Bible, going to prayer service, paying tithes and offerings, and giving a tenth of your time and talents. Yet, you still wonder why you can't get things right. I'll let you in on a secret. Men and women haven't gotten it right because you have no clue what happened in the Garden. What happened then affects you now, and you suffer from the consequences.

"Oh, there I go again, getting ahead of myself. I get so excited when I think about how I have succeeded in deceiving you. Like Adam and Eve, you don't know the bigger picture. You are naïve to believe that my original form looked like a snake. Not so. I had it going on. There was not a more beautiful being ever created. The prophet Ezekiel describes me perfectly, and if you read your Bible, you would know that. And here's a bonus: inside the Bible is all the ammunition you need to use against me. But I don't have to worry about that because you don't read your Bible," he added mockingly.

She-Devil reminiscently interjects, "Moving right along. Yes, Ezekiel said you were a seal of perfection, adorned with the most elaborate jewels: Sardius, Topaz, Diamond, Beryl, Onyx, Jasper, Sapphire, Turquoise, and Emerald with Gold.

Every precious stone was your covering. You were pleasing to the eye, beautiful, fine, and full of wisdom with no blemishes. Eden was your home, the Garden of God."

Master Satan adds, "Remember, I was a great musician. Special instruments were prepared for me when God created me. I was the anointed Angel of Light. The word of God says that I resided on the Holy Mountain of God. I had authority, and I was so magnificent I walked on fiery stones. I, like another character," he said with a smirk, "could have been considered the apple of God's eye."

Master Satan continues, "Yes, God, I am speaking to You. I had it all until you claimed you found iniquity in me. Do you know what iniquity is?" he asks rhetorically. "Although You define it as evil, wicked, and not righteous. I describe myself differently; I am a free agent, independent, and able to do as I please."

She-Devil looks up and says to God, "What were You thinking? In Your superiority, did You really think you could contain me in all my beauty? I think not. In my greatness and wisdom, I have others willing to follow me. Why despise me? You created me. Yes, God, you created evil."

You see, balance must be in the equation. God created all things, so if He created good, He must have created evil.

God's voice resounded in the atmosphere as He said, "You seem to have amnesia, so let me remind you that I am the giver of every perfect gift. Yes, I created you beautiful, but you became arrogant and turned into a violent ugly being and due to your selfish motives, I removed you from the

Holy Mountain of God, cursed you above every beast, and sent you to the ground."

4. THE FALL OF SATAN

The Fall of Satan happened in the Garden of Eden after the Creation of Man and Woman. Since then, Satan has come in various forms. You see, he can even replicate himself into a woman, the She-Devil.

"What was I thinking? I never thought the Father, Son, and Holy Spirit (the Trinity) would go that far and replace me with some second creation. How dare They! I was the most beautiful creation. When God created me, all other creations stopped and gazed at what a perfectly formed being I was. All of this should have been mine. I made one mistake by exercising my right to explore my options.

Nevertheless, all is not lost because I have my following, my faithful Imps. God thinks He's the only one who can create. What an egotistical B–." "Don't you say it, Master of Lies," the Imps interrupted, cackling before She-Devil could finish her sentence.

"The Trinity must get a hard-on looking at their so-called creation. The wind, the waves, the animals, the vegetation, and now their latest creation, man and woman. I watched God communing with Adam, giving him instructions, and having a holy fellowship. God never gave me any helpmate. It would have been nice to have someone who was part of me. What did God think when he made me? I am a chameleon-like entity. What a hell I have been living in. Why couldn't He be satisfied with me? What were They thinking, creating man and woman? Were They trying to replace me? I think not!" humphed She-Devil, answering herself with a sinister laugh.

"I will show God how *im*perfect His new creation is. I want Adam and Eve to fall just like me. That will surely get to God. It will be worthwhile if I can use God's precious man and woman to get to Him. Nothing personal against Adam and Eve; I have a greater plan.

"If I can use man and woman, I can break loose. This solitary confinement is a 'mother.' God defrocked me from my position, and now it seems like He is giving it to someone else. He restricted me to this tree, and Eden has turned from a paradise into a satanic graveyard. However, God's one mistake was giving them free will."

The Satan Trio laughs, and Master Satan chimes in, "Yes. Eve does not recognize that there are good and bad consequences to everything we do. She doesn't know that one encounter with me can cause negative repercussions for many generations. It's all about choices."

"From prior experience, I know that Adam might prove challenging to manipulate. Therefore, I will work on his strength by conversing with Eve while he communes with God."

Doesn't entrapment always start with a conversation, and doesn't that conversation always start with a question?

"I will beguile Eve into thinking that what she is doing is good for them. Remember, the fruit on that tree looked no different than the others, so I will subtly turn the truth around, trusting that I can get her to listen to the wrong voice. I'll use seduction to distract her from all the blessings of the Garden. If I can get her to focus on that one tree, I will have her. I might have to indulge her in several conversations, but my diligence will pay off, and I will use fear, envy, and distrust as my constant weapons.

15 Thou wast perfect in thy ways from the day that thou wast created, till iniquity was found in thee. 16 By the multitude of thy merchandise they have filled the midst of thee with violence, and thou hast sinned: therefore I will cast thee as profane out of the mountain of God: and I will destroy thee, O covering cherub, from the midst of the stones of fire.

(Ezekiel 28:15-16, KJV)

5. THE SEDUCTION AND MANIPULATION

Master Satan: "You wonder why I went to such lengths to deceive Adam and Eve. I might as well come clean because I have nothing to lose. I won. My plan worked and is still working. My 'why' is two-fold. I was envious of Adam and Eve for several reasons. Adam and Eve had one another. I have other demons, but there is no comparison to the connection a man and a woman have with each other," he reasons remorsefully. "I didn't know then, but I know now that God loves man and woman so much, He offered them forgiveness and mercy. Forgiveness through Jesus and mercy through not allowing them to live in that sinful state forever," he continues tearfully. "But I don't need your pity. You do not matter to me. You are merely a pawn in my game plan. If I influence you to be continuously disobedient to God, I ultimately get back at Him."

The Imps agreed, "Yeah, you know that's right. Get back at God!"

Flunky-Deceiver: "Why wasn't I given grace or mercy!? That's why I get so much pleasure from having man and woman in chaos against each other. Divide and conquer is always my modus operandi, and I am quite masterful at deceiving and manipulating information on multiple levels. To quote an old proverb, 'Misery loves company.'

"I am masterful at knowing the word of God and ingenious at helping you misinterpret it. I also skillfully misguide you to focus on what's wrong in your relationship so that you cannot appreciate what you have.

"If I may brag a moment, I think my biggest strength is distorting what you hear. That was my primary tactic with Eve."

Master Satan interjects: "Before you go into that, let me take a moment to introduce my staff officially and thank them for how they've assisted me in deceiving Adam and Eve, and ultimately mankind. Job well done, my faithful servants! Even Christ needed help. Jesus had Peter, James, and John in His inner circle, and I have my trustworthy inner circle.

"Although all my staff could not be here today because they are working on other assignments, I will introduce you to the main ones who have made the destruction of man and woman possible. They will address you briefly to outline their job descriptions. You will hear from the Demon of Envy, Demon of Distrust, and Demon of Fear, but first, we will start with my special assistant, the SHOULDER-DEMON."

"I was going to introduce my staff as Angels initially, but I did not want to misrepresent them, so I thought Demons would be more befitting. However, I need you to know that all of us are Angels; we are just Fallen-Angels. With that said, speak your piece Shoulder-Demon."

Shoulder-Demon: "I don't require a special introduction since I am always around. Unfortunately, humankind never acknowledges my presence due to their lack of spiritual awareness. So, let's check-in. Have your thoughts been contrary and confusing lately? Was one voice telling you logically that you should do one thing, and then another voice telling you not to? If so, that's where I come in. I make you think you are making rational decisions, but the reality is that the other voice challenging you to a higher level is God, leading you to where He wants you to go.

"Do you think I could keep my job if I allowed you to do what God wanted you to do? The ear is a powerful tool, and with me in your ear, you get stuck in your head overthinking and counteracting. It's easier with women because I have more to work with since they have so many thoughts and emotions going on at one time. A Shoulder-Demon's responsibility is to whisper in your ear and plant some of the following thoughts in your head:

- Thought-1: That doesn't make sense.
- Thought-2: Yeah, my husband told me that God told him I should stay home full time with the children, but God didn't tell me that.

- Thought-3: He wants me to stay home and depend on him. But I am an independent woman.
- Thought-4: He is talking about why he's so upset; I wish he would hurry up and finish so that I can make my point.
- Thought-5: That B@%#*, wearing that dress; she's trying to steal my man.

Conflicting thoughts and voices go through your head continuously. Whose voice are you listening to? God's or Demons'?

"Have you ever walked into a restaurant and saw your man dining with another woman? Or better yet, has someone come back to you and reported that they saw your man in a restaurant with an attractive woman? Whose voice did you hear? Did you hear the rational voice telling you that the woman in the restaurant could be a relative, a friend, or his employer? If you listened to the voice of reason, I wouldn't be any good at my job, now would I? I'm the deceptively sophisticated voice nudging you to hear, "Oh, he must be cheating on me!" I love whispering in your ear. I whispered in Eve's ear while my boss (Master Satan) interacted with her. I reiterated that she would not die eating fruit from that tree but would surely be like God, knowing good and evil. She couldn't resist.

"And don't think I only tempt women. I told you I am good at what I do. I also mislead men, but I work with them differently. Men need logic and very few words; you can get them if you communicate in a logical headlines style.

"I deceived Adam with faulty reasoning. Adam reasoned, 'The woman God gave me. If God gave me this woman, why would she give me anything that is not good for us? That fruit looked no different than the fruits from the other trees.'

"Remember, when the woman saw that the tree was good for food, and it would make her wise, she ate and gave it to her husband, and he ate. Adam reasoned about being wise." *Who or what are you listening to?*

The Demon of Envy speaks up: "It makes me mad when humans keep confusing me with jealousy. Let me set the record straight. Jealousy is suspicious and inflamed with anger at a rival. If I displayed jealous actions, it would suggest that competition is involved. But I need not compete with other spirits, for I am a very distinct spirit and stand on my own. The spirit of envy is rooted in the resentment of another's advantage. Envy is a more appropriate word to describe me.

"I was with God from the foundation of the world. When he created man from the dust of the ground, I looked in amazement at what he was doing. While watching God's love and creativity in making this man, I imagined that he probably did the same when he created us.

"While sitting in the pews on Sundays, I hear the preacher saying, 'God is always the God of another chance.' Where is my second chance? Since God didn't give me one, I do whatever I can to ensure that man won't get another chance. If I can have man and woman mess up often or badly enough, maybe God will get fed up and revoke Cavalry, canceling their second chances as He did with me.

"One way or another, I will get back at God through man and woman by any means necessary. If man and woman keep following my lead, they will become extinct. Maybe then, God will come to redeem me. Considering the beauty and splendor I once had, maybe the third creation will be bigger and better, and God will correct this miscarriage of justice."

The Demon of Distrust asks, "I keep hearing men and women say they need someone they can trust. But what is trust?"

The Shoulder-Demon responds, "Trust is being able to believe what your partner says is true, and he or she will always have your back."

The Demon of Fear adds, "Trust is knowing that your partner will always be there for you and is your covering. Trust believes that your partner will always be faithful."

The Shoulder-Demon continues, "Trust is that and a little more. To be effective in having man and woman distrust each other, we must be proficient in knowing what trust is. Trust is faith. It is not tangible, but you believe that it exists. It is confidence in the truth that whatever is being said or done is authentic. Trust is assured expectation and true commitment. Belief in knowing without any doubt. Peace in a person's decisions. Knowing that they have your best interest in mind. You will never have a restless night because you know that the other person is taking care of their responsibilities."

"Thanks for the trust breakdown, comrades," responded the Demon of Distrust. "I may not have known the full scope of trust, but I'm an expert on DISTRUST. I placed the spirit of distrust in Eve while she talked to our boss (Master Satan). While the Shoulder-Demon was planting thoughts in her head to lead her to the Fall, I subtly made Eve think that Adam couldn't manage things independently of God. I had her question his ability to think for himself. Questions are so effective. When I finished with her, she doubted everything." *What is the source of your doubt?*

The Demon of Fear shares his truth: "2 Timothy 1:7 says that God has not given you the spirit of fear, but of power, love, and a sound mind. Well, that's because it's my job to sow seeds of fear and insecurity. Call me FEAR. I will always have you focus on the limitations, and then I compound them, so they appear magnified. For example, if water spills, I compound it into a flood. When someone smiles in your direction, I compound it to make you think they're laughing at you. If your job offers a promotion, I compound it to make you feel you're inadequate and will fail. In addition to the compounding, I poison your mind and every fiber in your body and spirit to paralyze you. After the paralysis sets in, you are no good to yourself or anyone else.

"The spirit of fear also shows up as doubt, which you rationalize by saying: 'I'm playing it safe.' Do you not recognize that I cleverly utilize procrastination, another aspect of paralysis? Have you ever found yourself feeling like you shoulda, woulda, coulda? Are those your famous last words? Guess who was responsible for that? No need to feel bad for your failure; you are not alone.

"Adam and Eve were in an ideal state of provision and contentment. They had beautiful rivers surrounding Eden, perfect fellowship with God and the animals, and delicious fruit to eat from majestic trees. I compounded the fear of not eating from that one forbidden tree in the middle of the Garden.

"I, the Demon of Fear itself, made man and woman fear that they would not be wise; I made them afraid that they would be missing out on something if they did not eat from the tree of good and evil."

6. THE ART OF WAR WITH THE ENEMY

Master Satan: "I'm here because I am sick and tired of all the misunderstandings surrounding the Fall. Men blaming women. Women blaming men. Some even speculate that Adam and Eve tried to pass the buck when God confronted them. Adam said, 'The woman you gave me.' And Eve said, 'The serpent deceived me.' Despite their failings, I want to clarify my position by stating that when I messed up, my raison d'etra became to make man and woman continually mess up; this is the true purpose of my existence."

Flunky-Deceiver: "I've also heard it said that if Eve hadn't eaten from that tree, we would still live in the Garden. However, allow me to set the record straight. In some ways, I am like God. No one takes my glory. My passion for destroying Adam and Eve didn't originate with me hating man and woman. I wasn't personally. Let me explain:

"As a parent, you will feel strongly disturbed if someone messes with your child or does something sinister to destroy them. It is the same way with Adam and Eve and their descendants. Now that they have transitioned into ancestors, I get pleasure from messing with their descendants. Especially since this nagging bible passage in Psalm 8:4-6, NIV continues to haunt me, 'What is mankind that You are mindful of them? And human beings that You care for them? You have made them a little lower than the angels and crowned them with glory and honor. You made them rulers over the works of your hands; You have put everything under their feet.'"

She-Devil: "Why was a rib taken from Adam? I never had a rib. A rib could be helpful to a spirit like me. A rib taken from Adam's side must symbolically mean that God intended woman to always be by man's side since God created woman to be a helpmate for man. Anyway, the bottom line is that both Adam and Eve were victims. See, I tell the truth but with a slight slant.

"Adam was one phenomenal brother. He was Jesus' forerunner. Today, Adam would have been called the epitome of a Black Man, spiritual, made in God's image and likeness, handsome, built to perfection. He was God's main man, exceptional in every endeavor. Adam seriously cultivated a consistent and wholesome communion with God that included study, fellowship with God and nature, and worship with his wife."

Master Satan: "How ironic that after the Fall, God cursed me to crawl on my belly and eat dust all the days of my life. Yet, He created Adam from the dust of the ground but punished me to eat it! Also, note that God called me a serpent because of my character, not because I looked like a snake. I, as a serpent, was charming in my deceit and deadliness.

"Now, if you, man and woman, pay attention to what we are telling you, you will stop blaming each other. I was also there with Adam and Eve and the animals before the seduction. If Eve had listened to what is known today as women's intuition, she could have realized that there was always a peculiar presence occupying that forbidden tree in the center of the Garden."

Shoulder-Demon: "But, all she knew was that Adam and God said it was off-limits. She seemed okay with their instructions initially, but that was before the seduction.

Do you know what it's like for someone to seduce you? After the seduction, you sit and wonder why you fell for it. One moment of seduction could lead to an eternity of hell.

"The serpent deceived Eve. God had made her for Adam, yet Eve was vulnerable to seduction by someone other than her husband. How about that? But in her defense, God never spoke to Eve directly. He always spoke to her through Adam, which turned out to be a big mistake. Eve never bargained for the likes of me, the ultimate seducer."

Eve transparently discloses her truth and viewpoint: "Honestly speaking, the seduction wasn't unpleasant. He was easy on the eyes. His words and his posture ignited something sensual in me. His suggested touch was enough. The foreplay was the enticement of the fruit. The intentional misrepresentation of the phrase, 'Did God Say?' was the bait on the hook for me. I didn't have a relationship with God; my man did. In my innocence, I thought doing this might be a way for me to have a personal relationship with God. Satan seemingly made disobedience make sense. Why did he have to seduce me? Was it because I was weak?

NO! Don't get it twisted. There is nothing weak about a woman, and God wouldn't give man anything weak to help him. A woman endures childbirth and works in this white man-dominated world. She cooks, cleans, plans parties, goes to PTA meetings, and meets her children's needs. She is assertive when needed and sensitive, too; she makes time for God and takes care of her man's needs physically, spiritually, emotionally, and mentally. Women are strong, inside and out.

"Let me start from the beginning. As you can imagine, everything was incredibly serene and beautiful in the Garden; and Adam was God's chief priest. I did not have to worry about where my next meal was coming from because God gave us access to everything. There was good food in the Garden with plenty of fresh fruits and vegetables. I miss picking various types of fruit from the trees in the mornings.

"Fashion and clothing were never a concern because God gave me the most attractive fashion statement in my beautiful Black Body. I had no insecurities or shame about my nakedness because God gave me only positive thoughts about myself. God made it clear that He stamped my body with His seal of approval, and it read 'Very Good.'

"I had everything but took it all for granted. Have you ever asked yourself, 'What if?' What if I didn't entertain Satan when he approached me? What if Adam and I took the time to pray and discuss the pros and cons before eating the fruit? Or even better, what if we went and talked directly to God?"

Adam shares his perspective: "There is a time and season for everything. Nothing happens before its time. Eve was given to me when I was ready for her. God made me first for Himself, and we spiritually courted each other 24-hours a day. But as God watched my overall interactions with the animals and nature, He realized a need that I didn't even know I had. I needed a suitable companion to meet every level of my being, mentally, physically, emotionally, and spiritually. In recognizing that I needed a helpmate, God made Eve from me for me. An extraordinary gift. God did not want me to misuse His gift, so he presented Eve to me when I was ready for her.

Every good and perfect gift comes from God. Are you grateful for your gift(s)?

"My readiness had nothing to do with Eve. I had to bond with God in preparation for receiving my gift. I had no distractions because there was only God to communicate with intelligently. After developing my spiritual relationship, I was ready for my helpmate, companion, wife, and lover.

"When I first saw Eve, she was all that. Allow me to get caught up in the moment and describe this exquisite example of true beauty. Eve's skin was golden with natural tints and highlights applied by the sun. She was a voluptuous woman with a regal posture and curves I remember all so well. Eve exhibited a variety of facial expressions and attitude tones, depending on whatever the weather or her mood was.

"On that dreadful day in the Garden, I saw Eve in ways I had not noticed since God first presented her. She was stunning to watch with her succulent amber lips, dimpled caramel cheeks, firm walnut-colored breasts, and hallelujah hips, whose sway rivaled the very rhythm of the universe. Her skin glowed silky soft, and her bright smile showed more radiantly. There was nothing artificial about Eve; she was completely authentic from the inside out. Her statuesque naked body held no imperfections, and her sweet disposition was wholesome, humble, and willing to serve our God and me.

Important Considerations for the Adams and Eves of Today:

Although life presents many distractions, you can successfully minimize or eliminate several distractions if you do the following:

1. *Intentionally prioritize your time with God.*
2. *Regularly engage in prayer, bible study, and fellowship as core ingredients to developing a personal and intimate bond with God.*
3. *During your time with God, also search your soul and listen. One man once said, "Work on your soul if you want a soulmate."*

What does your time with God look like?

Also, God made man with a purpose. God created us with specific assignments. There are no accidents, no coincidences. We were born to do a particular work, and no one else can do that work like you.

What happens if you don't accept or fulfill your assignment?

What is your purpose?

²²For as in Adam all die, even so in Christ shall all be made alive.

(1 Corinthians 15:22, KJV)

7. THE SOLUTION

Master Satan: "I don't want you to think that God created man and woman, and boom, on the eighth day, they sinned. Adam and Eve had a good thing going on for a long time. They were in perfect fellowship with nature and their God. There were no tensions between Adam and Eve, nor were there any tensions between the entities of nature. Adam understood his role and responsibility, and so did Eve. I watched in amazement and envy as Eve got pleasure from preparing meals for Adam. Adam appeared to be appreciative. They complemented each other. Adam was Eve's mirror, reflecting what she could not see in herself, and Eve was Adam's mirror, reflecting what he could not see in himself."

She-Devil: "Before I deceived them, I would observe Eve not saying a word. However, her smile was enough for Adam to know that she was on the same page with him. I, who had never experienced a helpmate, became outraged that simply holding each other seemed enough for Adam and Eve. Adam got on his knees and thanked God in Eve's presence for blessing him with such fortified, magnificent excellence of beautiful Black Womanhood. In observing this couple's connection, I told the other demons, enough is enough!"

Flunky-Deceiver: "Yes, She-Devil. Adam and Eve had a full range of happiness in the Garden. And it was time to rock that boat. That day in the Garden was not the first time I tempted Eve. I was persistent every day, using innovative ways to lure her until the perfect opportunity arose. I know to always zero in on the vulnerable points. My packaging is not important, but my motives and intent remain the same.

"Eve did go to Adam about my interactions with her. The exchange between the two of them was quite entertaining. Adam told Eve to ignore me, stay away, and leave it alone. But I whispered into Eve's ear, 'Who does Adam think he is? Is he ignoring your feelings?' How can one ignore a presence that is always there?"

Adam reflectively shares: "Things were going just fine until he showed up. I watched the way that serpent interacted with my woman. She smiled, and he went to work. He knew just the right things to say. When she gave me that piece of fruit, it looked no different from all the other fruit we had eaten, so I went along with the program. What a mistake."

The Satan Trio: "We are The Surprise Witness, and we are wrapping it up as we have some more lives to ruin. You may wonder why we took the time to school humans about what took place in the Garden. The reason is that we've studied man and woman and know that you will not listen. They should have titled Genesis 3 – *How Satan Deceived Man and Woman* instead of *The Fall of Man and Woman*."

She-Devil: "I'm good because I don't have to use any new techniques; the old ones work just fine. My favorite ploy is using third parties. Think about who that third party was that ruined your relationship. I was the third party with Adam and Eve. However, I also use other third parties, like Jobs, Money, Family, and Friends. Introducing a member of the opposite sex into the scenario is my backup third party."

Shoulder Demon: "God and I have been going at it for a long time. When Adam and Eve sinned, I was cursed, but it was worth grieving God."

Demon of Envy: "When your relationship breaks up, I get back at God. When your children use drugs, I mess with God. When Black males become part of the prison industrial complex, I mess with God. When there are pandemics and diseases, I continue to work out my assignment getting back at God. However, there is something so simple that you can do to prevent me from messing with God. **Remember that you need each other and act like it**.

The Satan Trio: "It wasn't Adam's or Eve's fault. If you must blame somebody, blame us for seizing the opportunity to ruin humanity.

"We will leave you with one more source to remind you that you need each other. Genesis 4:7 says if you do well, you will be accepted. And if you don't, sin lies at the door; and it desires you. But you should rule over it." *What sin is lying at your door?*

God's unconditional gift of love provides us with the power and the victory to be overcomers in all things. He declares, "I will give humankind the ultimate gift. Nothing will be able to erase this, not disobedience, temptation, or the eating from any tree. I will send my only Son, Jesus, to shed His redeeming blood. He will take on human form indwelled with divinity. This provision is my guarantee that eternal life will always be available for humanity. Even if man and woman sin again, the blood that Jesus sheds will cover a multitude of sins, and nothing will ever separate humankind from the Love of God.

The Satan Trio says to each other, "If they get this, death and the hellish pit will be our home for eternity. Hopefully, they forget this last piece of wisdom:

The mind has a strong drive to correct and re-correct itself over a period of time if it can touch some substantial original historical base." *(From the Willie Lynch Letter- a speech given by a supposed 18th century white Jamaican slave owner detailing how Virginia slave owners could better keep their slaves in check using divisive psychological means).*

What would have happened if Adam and Eve had eaten from the tree of life?

Where do we go from here?

"⁸ Be sober, be vigilant; because your adversary the devil, as a roaring lion, walketh about, seeking whom he may devour:

⁹ Whom resist steadfast in the faith, knowing that the same afflictions are accomplished in your brethren that are in the world.

¹⁰ But the God of all grace, who hath called us unto his eternal glory by Christ Jesus, after that ye have suffered a while, make you perfect, stablish, strengthen, settle you."

(1 Peter 5:8-10, KJV)

ABOUT THE CONCEPT VISIONARY

Rev. Dr. Johnny Ray Youngblood spent 35 years (1974-2009) at St. Paul Community Baptist Church in Brooklyn, New York, also known as "Church Unusual," and holds the honorary title of Pastor Emeritus.

Rev. Dr. Youngblood continues to maintain a non-traditional approach to ministry. His prior accomplishments include transformational work with Black Men and Women, the Maafa Ministry, and his instrumental partnership with the East Brooklyn Congregations (EBC), building the Nehemiah homes.

Samuel G. Freedman chronicled the dynamic ministry of man and church in the 1994 publication "Upon This Rock: The Miracles of a Black Church."

During Rev. Dr. Johnny Ray Youngblood's tenure at St. Paul Community Baptist Church, he created the Think Tank Nucleus Group to study and dissect the Genesis story of Adam and Eve. His vision was that Satan would tell the story of what took place in the Garden of Eden.

In 2001, Rev. Dr. Youngblood became the Executive Pastor/Spiritual Engineer of Mount Pisgah Baptist Church.

On January 19, 2020, the Catholic and Apostolic Church of Jesus Christ our Lord conducted **Bishop** Dr. Johnny Ray Youngblood's ordination and consecration at the Pilgrim Baptist Church in Brooklyn.

ABOUT THE AUTHOR

Author Linda Lee Murrell has committed her life to the Ministry of Jesus Christ for more than 35 years. She is a prayer intercessor and a leader in the Women's Ministry at St. Paul Community Baptist Church. Linda has facilitated workshops on singleness and educated and trained new leadership.

Linda feels that it is a privilege to be part of a body of Christ that implements programming that will transform women's lives from the womb to over 90. Through partnering with her Pastor, Rev. Dr. David K. Brawley, infinite possibilities have taken place within the ministry.

In addition, Linda is a licensed social worker and has worked for 34 years in City Government. Linda has learned significant professional and spiritual lessons in her purpose-filled family and community work.